For my grandchildren: Khylee, Indya, Skyler, Myles, Faith, and Kiersten

When your parents were very small, I used to special-order Patricia McKissack's children's books for them to enjoy. I would read aloud to them each night while they cuddled up in my arms. Who knew that one day I would illustrate her picture book and be able to share this wonderful legacy with the children of my children!

I have learned that dreams really do come true and that what God has for you is for you. I pray that you treasure and believe that no matter where you find yourself in this world, God will find you and bestow upon you all that is planned for your life. Your mission is to be ready and say YES.

May your love of reading always catch you with a book in hand.

From my heart to yours,

Grandma April

And to Patricia: Although you're no longer with us and we didn't have an opportunity to meet prior to your passing, I truly felt your spirit was present while re-creating your story through pictures. Your work has been an inspiration to me, and I thank God for the opportunity to be a part of your last gift of storytelling through the written word. May God's peace and love continue to rest upon you, and may your voice be forever remembered in the hearts of children everywhere.

....

Text copyright © 2019 by Patricia C. McKissack

Jacket art and interior illustrations copyright © 2019 by April Harrison

All rights reserved. Published in the United States by Schwartz & Wade Books, an imprint of Random House Children's Books, a division of Penguin Random House LLC, New York.

Schwartz & Wade Books and the colophon are trademarks of Penguin Random House LLC.

Visit us on the Web! rhcbooks.com

Educators and librarians, for a variety of teaching tools, visit us at RHTeachersLibrarians.com

Library of Congress Cataloging-in-Publication Data is available upon request.

ISBN 978-0-375-83615-2 (trade)

ISBN 978-0-375-93615-9 (glb)

ISBN 978-0-375-98800-4 (ebook)

The text of this book is set in Adobe Caslon Pro.

The illustrations were rendered in mixed media, including acrylics, collage, art pens, and found objects.

MANUFACTURED IN CHINA

2 4 6 8 10 9 7 5 3 1

First Edition

WHAT IS GIVEN from the HEART

by

Patricia C. McKissack

....

illustrated by

April Harrison

schwartz & wade books · new york

Come June, we lost the farm and moved to a run-down shotgun house in the Bottoms.

On Friday the thirteenth, it rained frogs; everything flooded, and Smitty, my dog, disappeared.

"Misery loves company," Mama said, shaking her head as she swept water out the back door. I hugged her up close, the way I always did when she was sad or I was scared.

"Long as we have our health and strength, we are blessed, James Otis," Mama said, tryin' to sound brave. But things didn't get any better.

We got an early snowfall in November and Christmas

was skimpy, but we made it through to the new year.

'Fore I realized, February was upon us, with Valentine's Day just two weeks away.

One Sunday, Reverend Dennis made an announcement during services. "Just as we always do, we'll be delivering love boxes to needy folk in our community," he said. "Irene Temple and her little girl have lost everything in a fire. We must add them to our list. Next week, bring whatever you think might be useful to them. Remember, *what is given from the heart reaches the heart.*"

"James Otis, we need to help out," Mama said on the cold walk home.

I came back with "How we gon' do that, Mama? We aine got nothing ourselves."

Mama kept right on talkin'. "Sister Bunch told me the daughter's name is Sarah. She's seven, two years younger than you. You can find a li'l bit of something for her, don't you think?"

I wasn't convinced. "What do I have that a li'l girl would want?"

"Now, now," said Mama. "Remember what Reverend Dennis said? 'What is given from the heart reaches the heart.'"

That night, I lay warm and toasty under one of Mama's quilts. Still, it made me tremble to think about fire taking away what little we did have. *What can I give Sarah to make up for all she's lost?* I wondered.

I considered the blue ribbon I'd won in the school spelling bee. Naw. The award was important to *me*, but it would mean nothing to her.

I looked over at my beautiful sparkling rock, the one I'd found down by the creek. But how would that help Sarah? You can't eat a rock.

Unable to come up with anything good, I pulled the covers over my head and drifted off to sleep.

Come morning, I found Mama in the kitchen, busy sewing.

"I know if we had a fire, I would miss my aprons," Mama explained.

"So I've decided to make Mrs. Temple one."

"But, Mama, you're using your white tablecloth, the only nice

thing you have!"

"James Otis, I'm stitchin' with a loving heart. My hope is that this apron will give as much joy to Mrs. Temple as the tablecloth has given me."

Mama's smile was a welcome sight.

That made me study harder on what I could contribute.

Maybe Sarah would like something to play with, like my whistle from Dexter Benson's birthday party. But my spit was all over it. What about my crayons? I drew so many pictures with them, even though the black, pink, and dark blue were missing. No way. I couldn't give her used crayons. And I couldn't give her my pencil that was just a nub and not much eraser left either.

As time flew toward Valentine's Day, I fretted more and more. I considered giving Sarah a puzzle. It didn't bother me that two pieces were missing, but it might bother her. Unh-unh, that wouldn't do, not even with a bow on it. And neither would my capeless Superman Halloween costume.

Then I remembered my book, *Things That Roll*. Mama'd paid ten cents for it at the resale shop. I read it every night until I'd memorized each word, and then I drew pictures of all the stuff that rolled. Sarah might enjoy my book, I thought. But maybe she didn't like trucks and marbles and such. Still, it got me to thinking.

I gathered my crayons, my pencil, and some paper and got busy.

On the Sunday before Valentine's Day, we were off to church. Along the way Mama told me, "As usual, the trustees will deliver the love boxes to the homes of the needy. But Reverend Dennis has invited the Temples to receive theirs at Olive Chapel so they can meet the congregation."

The church was full. Mama beamed as she carefully placed the apron in the box.

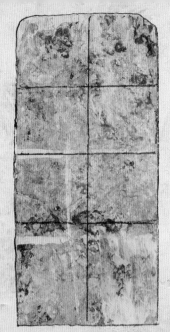

When we presented the Temples with their love box, filled with all kinds of clothing, food, tools, and toys, Mrs. Temple was overcome with emotion. The congregation shouted "Amen."

Even so, Sarah seemed sad and afraid. She clung to her mama's arm and hid her face.

I walked over to where they were standing. "Hi, Sarah," I said, sounding cheery-like. "My name is James Otis, and I'm pleased to meet you."

"Same to you," she answered, looking at her feet.

"Here," I said, handing her my gift. "I wrote it, drew the pictures, and put it together by myself—just for you."

Sarah managed a smile as she stared at the book I'd made. Then, real slow-like, she read the cover: "'*From My Heart to Your Heart*, by James Otis Petway.'"

"It's about a li'l girl named Sarah, and—"

"Don't tell me," she said. "I want to read about myself, by myself. I can't believe it!" she squealed. "A book about me." Then she covered her mouth to catch a giggle.

Seeing li'l Sarah happy made me happy, too. I laughed out loud.
"I put some hard words in, so you can look them up."

"You sound like my teacher!" Sarah pressed the book to her heart,
closed her eyes, and whispered, "Thank you, James Otis. I will keep
this book forever and ever."

Walking home, Mama held my hand. "The Temples looked very grateful,"
she said.

"I think we reached their hearts," I said.

Mama nodded. "I'm proud of you, James Otis."

"How come?" I asked.

"'Cause you're . . . *you.*"

In winter, night comes early. The sky was darkening, and it had started
to snow. I stuck my tongue out to catch a snowflake as Mama spun joyfully
round and round.

Suddenly, Mama stopped. "Look! There's something on our porch," she said.

I rushed ahead. And there it was—a love box had been

delivered to us.

And our hearts rejoiced!

Our hearts rejoiced!